NFL'S GREATEST PLAYERS

RUNNING BACKS

By Kevin Frederickson

Kaleidoscope
Minneapolis, MN

Your Front Row Seat to the Games

This edition first published in 2020 by Kaleidoscope Publishing, Inc.

For information regarding permission, write to
Kaleidoscope Publishing, Inc.
6012 Blue Circle Drive
Minnetonka, MN 55343

Library of Congress Control Number
2019939223

ISBN
978-1-64519-077-6 (library bound)
978-1-64494-173-7 (paperback)
978-1-64519-178-0 (ebook)

Printed in the United States of America.

TABLE OF
CONTENTS

CHAPTER 1

Marshawn Lynch was traded to Seattle in October of the 2010 season.

Beast Quake

Marshawn Lynch stands behind the quarterback. His hands are on his knees. He stands perfectly still, waiting for the play to start. It is the 2010 playoffs. Lynch's Seattle Seahawks need him to go into "beast mode."

Quarterback Matt Hasselbeck takes the **snap**. Lynch starts running to his left. Hasselbeck hands Lynch the ball. Now Lynch bursts straight ahead. His blockers try to clear a path. But the defensive players are closing in.

A New Orleans Saints defender tries to tackle Lynch around the waist. He grabs for Lynch's blue jersey. But the defender slips. Lynch keeps running forward.

Lynch gains more yards. Defenders keep reaching for him. But Lynch slips away. One grabs Lynch's foot. He nearly trips. But he keeps himself up.

Lynch gets farther down the field. Now another defender tries to wrap around Lynch. But Lynch shakes him off, too. Lynch keeps running. The crowd cheers louder as he goes.

Lynch runs to the right. The **end zone** is getting closer and closer. A defender runs next to Lynch. He tries grabbing Lynch around the shoulders. But Lynch sticks his arm out. He pushes the defender away. The defender goes flying. The crowd goes wild.

WHERE RUNNING BACKS LINE UP

The running back almost always lines up behind the quarterback. Sometimes they stand behind another blocker like a fullback. Other times they are alone in the backfield.

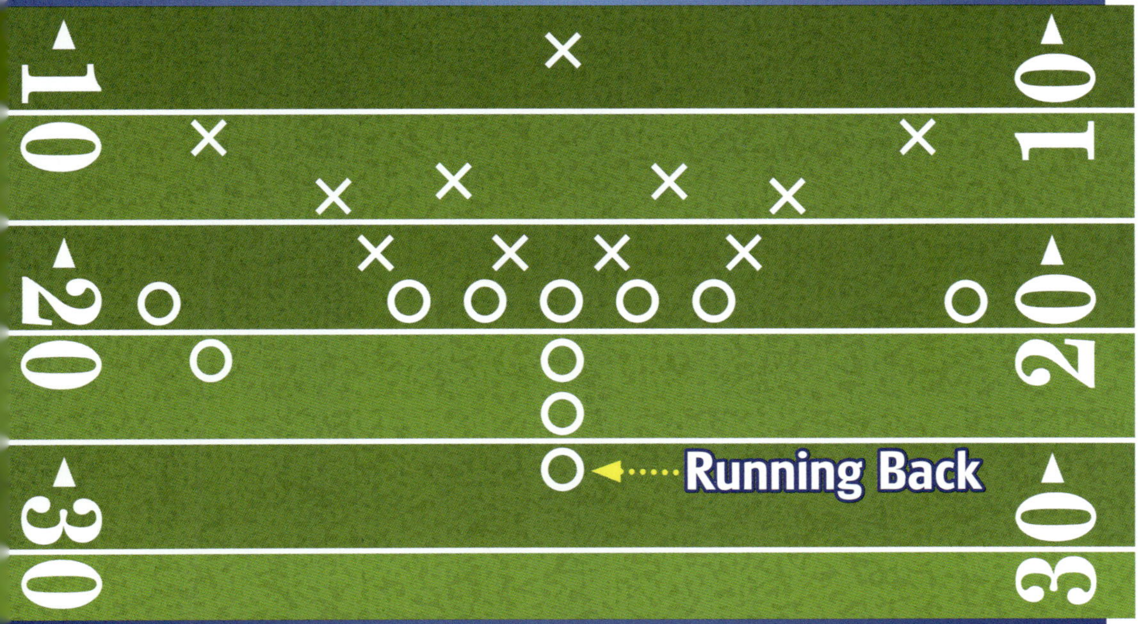

Lynch's teammates run ahead of him. One hits a defender out of the way. The other tries to find a defender to hit. Lynch is still running. He gets close to running out of bounds. A defender reaches out but can't get him. Lynch nears the end zone. He's almost there. Then, he turns around. He falls on his back into the end zone. Touchdown! Lynch ran 67 yards. The fans jumped around so much it felt like an earthquake.

Lynch runs away from a Saints defender on his way to the end zone.

Running backs have been important to teams for a long time. The National Football League (NFL) has seen many great ones.

FUN FACT
Marshawn Lynch loves candy, and sometimes he ate Skittles during games.

CHAPTER 2

All Shapes and Sizes

Adrian Peterson stood behind the quarterback. He waited for the ball. Defenders kept an eye on him. Peterson was big and strong. But he was also fast. The Minnesota Vikings running back could run right by a defender. Or he could run right over him.

Peterson got the ball. He sprinted through a gap. One defender reached to grab him. But Peterson was too strong. One arm could not bring him down. Peterson ran into another defender. He kept on going. Soon Peterson was running to an open space. He was loose!

FUN FACT
Adrian Peterson set the NFL record for rushing yards in a game with 296 in 2007.

Adrian Peterson is the Vikings' all-time leader in rushing yards with 11,747.

Marshall Faulk was named Most Valuable Player of the 2000 NFL season.

With no one left in his path, Peterson raced into the end zone. He dropped to his knees in celebration. Touchdown! Some running backs are small and fast. Others are big and strong. Peterson was a rare combo. He led the league in rushing yards three times. He was Most Valuable Player (MVP) in 2012.

Marshall Faulk was speedy. He starred for the St. Louis Rams. Faulk could make any defender miss. A bunch of Cleveland Browns missed him in a 1999 game. Faulk took the **handoff**. He ran up the middle. Then he stopped. In an instant, he cut to the right. Then he cut to the left. Suddenly, he was all alone. Faulk sprinted to the end zone. Touchdown!

Darren Sproles lined up behind the quarterback. Defenders could barely see him. He stood only 5-foot-6 (1.7 m). But his height helped him. He could slip through small openings. And he had the speed to get away.

Sproles could do more than run. He could also catch passes. He caught 86 in 2011. He carried the ball 87 times. Many running backs have this skill. It's another way for them to help their teams.

GOAL LINE GLORY

Not all running backs run long distances. Jerome Bettis was not fast. But he could plow through anybody. Bettis was a huge part of the Pittsburgh Steelers from 1996 to 2005. He was 5-foot-11 (1.8 m) and 243 pounds (110 kg). His nickname was "The Bus." He rarely broke big runs. But he got the yards his team needed.

Besides rushing and receiving, Darren Sproles also returned kicks.

CHAPTER 3

All-Time Greats

Jim Brown did not get tackled easily. Tall and strong, the Cleveland Browns legend ran up the field. A defender tried to grab Brown's leg. Brown stepped out of it. The defender fell to the ground. Brown kept running. He picked up speed.

Another defender reached for Brown's leg. But he grabbed nothing but air. Brown was gone. Brown was one of the game's first great running backs. He played in the 1950s and '60s.

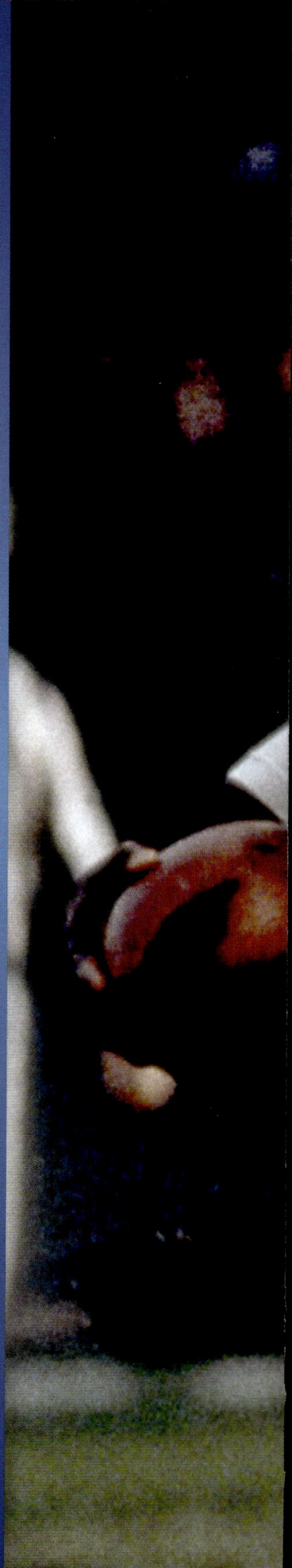

Jim Brown led the NFL in rushing in eight of the nine seasons he played.

The 1985 Chicago Bears did not have to score many points. They relied on their defense to win the Super Bowl. But they had one superstar on offense. Walter Payton scooted out to the right. Two defenders closed in. Payton **juked** to the left. Two more defenders tried to hit him. They only hit each other. Payton ran on for a 19-yard gain. Bears fans were used to amazing runs like that.

ANOTHER TYPE OF BACK

Running backs rely on the offensive line to create holes. But some teams rely on a second back to do that. This position is called the fullback. He runs ahead of the running back. One of the best ever was Lorenzo Neal. He played in San Diego with LaDainian Tomlinson. Neal rarely carried the ball himself. He never had more than 175 yards in a season. But he helped Tomlinson lead the league in rushing in 2006 and 2007.

Walter Payton played his entire career in Chicago and set more than 30 team records.

FUN FACT

Walter Payton's nickname was "Sweetness." It referred to both his kind personality and the sweet way he ran.

Emmitt Smith saw things other backs did not. The Dallas Cowboys running back could run through tiny holes. This helped him rack up tons of yards during the 1990s. Smith had a long career in the NFL. Teams kept giving him the ball. And they had good reason. Smith won an MVP Award and three Super Bowls. He ended his career with more rushing yards than anyone else in NFL history.

Defenders had to stay low when playing Barry Sanders. That's where Sanders made his living in the 1990s. He was harder to tackle. Often, defenders thought they had him. Then the next moment, he was gone. Another touchdown for the Detroit Lions legend.

TIMELINE OF TOP RUNNING BACKS

1955

Jim Brown,
Cleveland Browns
(1957–65)

1965

Walter Payton,
Chicago Bears
(1975–87)

1975

1985

Barry Sanders,
Detroit Lions
(1989–98)

Emmitt Smith,
Dallas Cowboys
(1990–2002),
Arizona Cardinals
(2003–04)

Marshall Faulk,
Indianapolis Colts
(1994–98),
St. Louis Rams
(1999–2006)

1995

Marshawn Lynch,
Buffalo Bills
(2007–10),
Seattle Seahawks
(2010–15),
Oakland Raiders
(2017–18)

Darren Sproles,
San Diego Chargers
(2005–10),
New Orleans Saints
(2011–13),
Philadelphia Eagles
(2014–18)

2005

Ezekiel Elliott,
Dallas Cowboys
(2016–)

2015

Alvin Kamara,
New Orleans Saints
(2017–)

Saquon Barkley,
New York Giants
(2018–)

2025

CHAPTER 4

A Group Effort

Alvin Kamara stood next to quarterback Drew Brees. Brees took the snap. Kamara ran to his right. But he did not take a handoff. Brees threw the ball to Kamara. Kamara caught it. He ran straight ahead. He rounded a defender. Finally, a defender tackled Kamara. It was a nice gain. Kamara ran to the **sideline**.

Mark Ingram, right, and Alvin Kamara, left, formed a powerful running back duo for the Saints.

Mark Ingram ran onto the field. He also lined up behind Brees. Brees handed the ball to Ingram. He ran straight ahead for a four-yard gain. Kamara and Ingram were both running backs for the New Orleans Saints. The Saints used each of them during games in 2018. Each provided different strengths. Together, they made for an elite pairing.

Ezekiel Elliott can run and catch, too. But he is best at running. Elliott was a star right away for the Dallas Cowboys. He led the league in rushing his **rookie** year in 2016. He did it again in 2018. He quickly became one of the top backs in the NFL.

Saquon Barkley was right behind Elliott in 2018. He had a lot to prove. The New York Giants **drafted** him second overall. Some thought he was not worth that high a pick. But Barkley proved them wrong. He saw holes open in the defense and had the speed to punch through them. He had a 68-yard touchdown in his first NFL game.

Ezekiel Elliott celebrates scoring a touchdown in 2016.

EZEKIEL ELLIOTT

CAREER STATS

Through the 2018 season

RECEIVING YARDS	1,199
RUSHING TOUCHDOWNS	28
RUSHING YARDS	4,048
YARDS PER ATTEMPT	4.7
RECEIVING TOUCHDOWNS	6

Saquon Barkley is an amazing athlete who is not afraid to leap over defenders if necessary.

The Giants were playing the Jacksonville Jaguars. It was the fourth quarter. The Giants trailed by 11. Barkley got the snap. He ran to his right. He broke a tackle. Then he broke another. Suddenly he was all alone. Only one Jaguar could catch him. He dived for Barkley's legs. But Barkley stepped high and over him. Touchdown!

That was just the start. Barkley quickly became one of the game's great young running backs. Some backs are fast. Some can catch. Some bash their way to big yards. The method doesn't matter. There are many ways to be a great NFL running back.

BEYOND THE BOOK

After reading the book, it's time to think about what you learned. Try the following exercises to jumpstart your ideas.

THINK

DIFFERENT SOURCES. Think about what types of sources you could find on running backs. What could you find in a library? What could you learn at a football stadium? What about an interview with a retired player? How could each of the sources be useful in its own way?

CREATE

PRIMARY SOURCES. A primary source is an original document, photograph, or interview. Make a list of different primary sources you might be able to find about Adrian Peterson. What new information might you learn from these sources?

SHARE

WHAT'S YOUR OPINION? In Chapter Four, the book says Saquon Barkley is one of the best young running backs in the NFL. Do you agree or disagree with this position? Use evidence from the text to support your answer. Share your position and evidence with a friend. Does your friend agree with you?

GROW

REAL-LIFE RESEARCH. What places could you visit to learn more about running backs? What other things could you learn while you were there?

RESEARCH NINJA

Visit www.ninjaresearcher.com/0776 to learn how to take your research skills and book report writing to the next level!

RESEARCH

DIGITAL LITERACY TOOLS

SEARCH LIKE A PRO
Learn about how to use search engines to find useful websites.

FACT OR FAKE?
Discover how you can tell a trusted website from an untrustworthy resource.

TEXT DETECTIVE
Explore how to zero in on the information you need most.

SHOW YOUR WORK
Research responsibly—learn how to cite sources.

WRITE

GET TO THE POINT
Learn how to express your main ideas.

PLAN OF ATTACK
Learn prewriting exercises and create an outline.

DOWNLOADABLE REPORT FORMS

Further Resources

BOOKS

Braun, Eric. *Football's Greatest Running Backs.* Capstone, 2015.

Hewson, Anthony K. *Todd Gurley.* Kaleidoscope, 2020.

Leventhal, Josh. *Running Backs.* Black Rabbit Books, 2017.

WEBSITES

FACTSURFER

Factsurfer.com gives you a safe, fun way to find more information.

1. Go to www.factsurfer.com.
2. Enter "Running Backs" into the search box and click 🔍.
3. Select your book cover to see a list of related websites.

Glossary

drafted: Players new to the league get drafted by pro teams and added to their rosters. Saquon Barkley was the second pick in the draft.

end zone: The end zone is where someone has to go to score a touchdown. Marshall Faulk sprinted ahead into the end zone for a touchdown.

handoff: In football, a handoff happens when one player gives the ball directly to another. Adrian Peterson got the handoff from the quarterback and ran downfield.

juked: In football, a defender gets juked when a player fakes going one way only to go the other way. Walter Payton juked to the left to avoid the defender.

rookie: A rookie is a professional athlete playing in his or her first year. Ezekiel Elliott led the NFL in rushing yards in his rookie year.

sideline: The sideline is the area alongside the playing field where coaches and players not currently playing stand. Marshawn Lynch ran to the sideline and sat on the bench.

snap: The snap is what starts a play when the center gives the ball to another player. Drew Brees took the snap and handed off to Alvin Kamara.

Index

PHOTO CREDITS

The images in this book are reproduced through the courtesy of: Margaret Bowles/AP Images, front cover (left), p. 3; Greg Trott/AP Images, front cover (center); Evan Pinkus/AP Images, front cover (right); EFKS/Shutterstock Images, front cover (background); Kevin Terrell/AP Images, pp. 4–5; dean bertoncelj/Shutterstock Images, pp. 6, 13, 21 (football); Red Line Editorial, pp. 7, 21 (timeline), 25 (chart); Ted S. Warren/AP Images, pp. 8–9; Jeff Bukowski/Shutterstock Images, pp. 10, 20, 27; Seth Perlman/AP Images, p. 11; Ben Margot/AP Images, p. 12; Paul Spinelli/ AP Images, pp. 14–15, 19; Tony Tomsic/AP Images, pp. 16, 16–17; NFL Photos/AP Images, pp. 22–23; Don Wright/AP Images, p. 24; Ron Jenkins/AP Images, p. 25 (Ezekiel Elliott); Bill Kostroun/AP Images, pp. 26–27; Carlos E. Santa Maria/Shutterstock Images, p. 30.

ABOUT THE AUTHOR

Kevin Frederickson is a freelance writer and editor from Ohio. He lives near Cincinnati with his golden doodle, Max.